Nothing Lasts Forever Anymore

Michael Lederer

Nothing Lasts Forever Anymore

With illustrations by Genia Chef

PalmArtPress
Berlin

Bibliografische Information der Deutschen Nationalbibliothek
Die Deutsche Nationalbibliothek verzeichnet diese Publikation in der Deutschen Nationalbibliografie; detaillierte bibliografische Daten sind im Internet über http://www.d-nb.de abrufbar.

ISBN: 978-3-941524-33-0

First Edition, Parsifal Ediciones, Barcelona, 1999, ISBN: 84-87265-98-7
Spanish Edition, Parsifal Ediciones, *Ya nada dura eternamente,* 1999, ISBN: 84-87265-99-5

PalmArtPress, 2013, Revised English Edition, ISBN: 978-3-941524-33-0
German Edition, 2013, *Nichts ist mehr für die Ewigkeit*, ISBN: 978-3-941524-32-3
German Edition eBook, 2013, ISBN: 978-3-941524-31-6
Front cover: Genia Chef, *Juan's World*, oil on panel, 1995
Illustrations: Genia Chef, pen and sepia ink with juice from Spanish olives, 1999
Editor: Catharine J. Nicely
Printed in Germany

Pfalzburger Str. 69, 10719 Berlin
www.palmartpress.com

For Nicholas

Preface

I wrote this book in 1984 – 85 when I was twenty-eight years old. It was a different Spain in a different world. No Internet, no mobile phones, no satellite dishes on rooftops. A young goatherd still pressed his flock through the little streets of La Herradura, the fishing village where I lived south of Granada. There were fishing boats with nets heaped beside them on the long pebble beach. On nights when there was no moon the light from the stars was so clear it cast shadows on the ground.

But all that was coming to a fast end. Along the Mediterranean coast, towering apartment buildings and hotels were sprouting up as fast as one could scream "Money!" It was not just a century or a millennium coming to a close. Things that once looked like they would last forever...family, faith, the rhythm of life, horizons...all of that was changing.

When I went back to visit La Herradura years later, most of those little boats were gone. The fishermen didn't mend nets or make fires on that beach anymore. The light from all the new buildings made the stars harder to see. And the goats were gone. Maybe the goatherd had become a real estate agent.

Michael Lederer

Berlin
2013

"All things must pass."

- *George Harrison*

GOOD NEWS

It began, at least, like any other day. The sun had not yet risen above the peaks of the Sierra Nevada, and only the white light from the moon and stars shone down on the little *cortijo*. The cock had already been crowing for an hour or so, and the crickets in the olive trees were chirping back and forth to one another.

Aurelio finished milking the two goats, and now he carried the milk in an old pail down the narrow pathway to the house. The rest of the family was still sleeping, and as he did every morning, so as not to wake them, the old man quietly put the pail down on the wooden table in the kitchen, turned and went back outside.

It was cool still, and he stopped just outside the door to make sure that the top button of his sweater was fastened. Then he walked back up the little pathway, past the barn and the chicken coop and the cages where the pigeons and rabbits were kept, until he came to the end of an old dry-stone wall. This wall had been built by Aurelio's grandfather nearly a hundred years before, and had at last, just recently, begun to crumble. The old man and his son, Juanma, knew that if they didn't mend it soon whole sections of the wall would be in danger of collapsing, and there had been plenty of talk of getting to it for some time. But as always there was more work on the *cortijo* than they and Concha, Juanma's wife, were able to handle, and so the wall for the time being had had to wait.

Aurelio turned now and left the path. Stepping carefully so as not to trip on the rubble, he made his way along the wall until he came to a spot where it was still fairly sturdy, and where the stones along the top were relatively smooth. Then he stopped. He pulled a little piece of cardboard from his rear pocket, unfolded it, laid it flat across the smoothest stone and sat. It was from this spot every morning that the old man loved to watch the sun rise. He shifted his weight around a bit until he found the most comfortable position, and crossed his arms to shield himself from the morning chill. Then he simply sat there, hardly moving, waiting for the sun.

In front of him, stretching down the hill and toward the sea, was the family's small olive orchard. As if in some sort of primordial challenge to the light from the moon and stars, each tree cast a long dark shadow onto the ground as if it were a kind of gauntlet. Aurelio's own shadow, meanwhile, fell behind him onto the other side of the wall where it skirted the edge of the family's little vineyard. It was from this vineyard that Aurelio and Juanma produced their *vino del terreno*, an unfortified, sherry-like wine of which the old man in particular was very proud.

Further up the hill, just beyond the vineyard, were three terraced rows of, respectively, avocado, lemon and blood-orange trees, while above and to the right of these stood the family's small almond grove. Altogether they were able to raise nearly everything they needed to survive. And what they couldn't provide for themselves, they bought with the money they earned by selling some of their olives, and most of their almonds, to the little market stalls in the nearby town of La Herradura.

For some time, as Aurelio sat there thinking, nearly everything in sight appeared to be one or another shade of blue. From the blackish blue of the Sierra Nevada silhouetted in the distance, to the pale blue of the whitewashed walls of the *cortijo*. Beyond the *cortijo* at the bottom of the hill the Mediterranean sea, the darkest blue of all, stretched out from the shore to the horizon, while in the distance the lighthouse across the bay at Torrenueva shot forth its intermittent beacon. A light from a small fishing boat would sometimes also pierce the darkness and, as if thrown by the hand of an unseen child, come skipping across the water like a stone.

Gradually at last one by one the stars began to disappear, the moon began to fade, and as if to take their place a wide array of colors began to spread out across the scene. The tops of the olive trees at first became a silvery gray, and then almost imperceptibly a muted green, while a fast-growing band of yellow and orange light appeared above the horizon. The night sky faded. It became pale, as here and there a small white cloud, already in the sun, turned to coral pink. Finally Aurelio could make out the red clay tiles on the roofs of the house and barn, and the red of the soil beneath his feet.

The air was beginning to get warmer now, and as

it warmed the smell of wild thyme that grew along the wall and on the terraced slope above the vineyard grew stronger. It was a smell that always took the old man back to his childhood. As a young boy he had often helped his mother gather wild thyme in the nearby hills. Aurelio breathed in deeply now, closing his eyes as if with eyes closed he could see the past more clearly.

He could see his mother, young and beautiful, clutching her apron and laughing over her shoulder as she would race him along the pathway to the very spot on the wall where he now sat. There they would both pause, catching their breaths before racing the final leg to the house. Sometimes he would win, though years later he realized that was only when she let him, for by the time his legs were long enough, and he was strong enough to win on his own, he was no longer spending his days helping his mother gather herbs. By then his very strength had led to other more strenuous chores, such as helping his father with the mule, or trimming dead branches from the olive trees.

As Aurelio's mind wandered back to the present, he noticed that the crickets in the olive trees had stopped their chirping, and in their stead now a variety of birds had begun to sing. The old man smiled to himself. For many, he realized, the day was just beginning. Meanwhile, from the bottom of the hill, as always, came the constant sound of the surf, as each wave wore away at the rocks along the shore, grain by grain by grain of sand, as if the sea was little more than a mighty hourglass.

Suddenly, as if in a violent dream there was a shattering explosion in the distance, followed by the roar of an engine. The birds stopped singing. Instinctively Aurelio's eyes shot open. His head jerked a little to the right as he looked out over the tops of the olive trees in the direction from which the noise had come. There he could see not far away, jutting out into the sea, a large hill called the Punta de la Mona.

For as long as Aurelio could remember, that hill had been called the Punta de la Concepcion. However some years earlier, for reasons the old man did not understand, the name had been changed. And now the hill itself had also changed. To be sure, familiar rows of ancient olive and Cypress trees still rose along the crest, and giant boulders, interspersed with prickly pear cacti with their sweet fruit, still dotted the hillside. Also the stone watchtower that had been built in the sixteenth century was still there, looming over it all. Only now, beginning just below the tower and stretching down the side of the hill to the edge of the sea, and even beyond the edge of the sea, was the site of a major urbanization development. A large crane, taller even than the tallest Cypress tree, stood at the center of a sprawling complex. There were other machines, and great pipes and coils of cable everywhere.

The sun was beginning to rise above the mountains now, and already scores of men in blue overalls were milling about like ants on an anthill. About a dozen of them were scrambling through the cloud of dust that hung over the spot they had just dynamited. Close by, another group of men was clustered around a great yellow bulldozer. One of those men had climbed up onto the bulldozer and it was this that, following the blast of the explosion, had sputtered and was now roaring. The noise bounced off the rocks as the echoes seemed to come from all directions.

Aurelio's eyes were still good despite his age, and he could see that the first group of men was preparing to detonate a second charge. Before the day was over, he knew, they would set off many such explosions. They had begun construction only the year before, and each day since Aurelio had been amazed at the speed with which they were able to build. It was as if time itself had somehow yielded to them.

He hadn't minded the development at first. It had been interesting, and even fun at times, to watch them dynamite the side of the hill, level and then clear it, pour their cement foundations, bring in electricity, water, sewage pipes and all the rest of it. One by one houses and apartments, like so many crops in the field, sprang up from the ground. But then one day the old man noticed something that upset him.

For as long as he could remember, Aurelio had know not a silence per se, because there had always been the sounds of the sea below, and the wind in the trees above, but rather a sort of calm that only now and then had been broken by a noise: a seagull squawking, a mule braying, or his own family going about the business of their day. But since they had begun constructing the urbanization, during days there was only noise that now and then was interrupted by a calm. Aurelio called this the "new calm," because even when the workmen were not working, at nights, during their midday breaks or on Sundays, he would find himself thinking of the noise, remembering it, and wondering when it would return. It was then, when the noise was inside him, that it was worst.

Sometimes in their rush the workmen had even begun to work on Sundays. The old man believed that was a sin, and when they did that he prayed for them. He also prayed, every morning and every night, for his little grandson, Jorge. That was because Jorge, at six years old, was having to grow up on the *cortijo* knowing nothing but the noise, and this "new calm."

When the old man had been a boy, aside from what even then had been good-sized towns like Motril, Salobreña and Almuñécar, most of the coast had consisted of small fishing villages and long open stretches dotted here and there with little family farms like theirs. One by one, however, the villages had become towns, the towns had turned into cities, and in order to accommodate foreign tourists who came from as far away as America to spend their summers basking in the Spanish sun, the entire coast from Gibraltar to Almeria and beyond was being urbanized. There were plenty of *cortijos* left in the interior, in the hills and on the mountains. But theirs was one of the last whose property actually extended to the sea. It saddened the old man to think that there were so few places left where little Jorge could gaze out at the water, listen to the wind, and know that old calm that Aurelio and Juanma could at least remember.

The sun was well above the mountains now and it began to grow hot quickly. That portion of the wall on which the old man sat was not in shade, so he took one last look around, stood, tucked the piece of cardboard back into his pocket and headed toward the house.

There had been a heavy rain the day before, and on the day before that as well. There was always extra work to be done after a rain. There would be fresh mushrooms in the field below the house and in the vineyard. There would be snails to gather. And later in the day, after the sun had warmed the side of the hill, there would be wild asparagus to pick. Again the old man smiled to himself. His family always ate especially well after a rain.

Furthermore, the timing could not have been better. In fact, Aurelio thought, it was as if it had been planned. Indeed, he was sure of it. For today was Good Friday, and like most of Spain the family was fasting, keeping what they ate to the essentials. Something as plain and simple, albeit as delicious, as fresh mushrooms could be eaten with impunity. The snails, however, a real delicacy, would have to be placed in a bowl of flour for a couple of days in order to flush themselves clean, and so would not be ready until the upcoming

Easter Sunday feast.

As he stepped up to the house now, Aurelio thought ahead to what he needed to do that day. After gathering the mushrooms and the snails, he and Jorge would sit together on the little patio behind the house and shell the last of the almonds left over from the year before. There were not many left, and they would be finished with those by the time the family sat down to eat. After eating, as always he and Jorge would take their *siestas*. And then in the afternoon, after they had picked the wild asparagus, and cleaned out the rabbit cage, the old man was going to teach his grandson how to whitewash.

Whitewashing was a job that Aurelio always looked forward to. In fact, of all the chores on the *cortijo* it had long been his favorite. It was such a joy to so quickly see such obvious results from one's labor. Not like planting a tree, for instance, then having to wait a year or two or even three before seeing the tree bear fruit. With whitewashing one only had to wait a day or so to see it dry and whiten. As Aurelio had grown older, he had come to appreciate that more and more.

This year, as it happened, he was looking forward to it more than ever. That was because this year Jorge was at last old enough to learn how it was done. The old man was looking forward to teaching him, just as his own grandfather had taught him how to whitewash some seventy or so years earlier. Jorge for his part was an eager student, and seemed as anxious to learn as his grandfather was to teach. In fact he had been talking about little else for over a week.

"When are you going to teach me how to white-wash, Abuelito?" he had been asking two, three, some-times four times a day.

"As soon as the last of the almonds are shelled," Aurelio would answer.

"And then?"

The old man would look at the boy and smile. "Then, my little one, you and I, we are going to make our house and our barn even more beautiful than they already are!"

Hearing that, Jorge would jump up, clap his hands and squeal with joy.

Aurelio paused now to take a careful look at the side of the house. The walls were yellowed and stained with dirt. The old man shook his head. Summer, fall and winter had gone by so quickly it seemed. It was hard to believe it was already a new spring, that they were in the middle of the Holy Week, and once again it was time to prepare for another year ahead.

Aurelio stepped up to the front door. On the wall hanging from a rusty nail was an old bucket. Inside the bucket was a plastic bag. He grabbed both, and as he did he could hear Concha's voice coming from inside the house. The adobe walls were thick though, so he could not make out what she was saying. Then with the bucket and bag in hand he headed down the pathway on the hunt for snails and mushrooms.

Inside the kitchen, Juanma was seated at the table drinking a glass of coffee. Jorge was sitting next to him. The boy was busy dipping a piece of bread into a bowl of hot goat's milk. Standing close by, leaning against the wooden counter, was Concha. She was looking at her husband and grinning.

"Oh Juanma," she said, eyes sparkling brightly, "I can't believe it! I just can't believe it's true! I was awake half the night. Did you hear me? I was looking out our window, thinking of how it's going to be!"

She was so excited. Everything she said seemed to have an exclamation mark after it. Juanma raised a quick finger to his lips and shot a glance at Jorge. Whatever Concha was about to say next, he didn't want it said in front of their son. Concha understood. She took one hand out of her apron pocket and held it over her mouth, as if she had to forcibly restrain herself from speaking.

Jorge was too busy eating to notice any of this. He had seen his grandfather walk past the window, and now was eating as fast as he could so he could go join him. The moment he finished he wiped his mouth clean with the back of his little hand and looked up.

"Mama, can I go out now and help Abuelito pick the mushrooms?"

"Of course you can."

Jorge pushed his chair back from the table, hopped to the floor and ran out. The moment he was out the door Concha crossed to her husband. She stood behind him, bent down and wrapped her arms around his shoulders.

"Oh Juanma, really I can't believe it's true. Tell me again what Vicente said to you."

"But I told you already last night."

"Tell me again. Please! I want to hear every word he said. *Every* word! And don't leave anything out."

Juanma laughed. "Alright. He said that... "

"No!" Concha cried. "Start at the beginning. The

very beginning. As if it was a story. A fairy tale. It *must* be a fairy tale, because I've tried and still I can't believe it's true. Convince me that it's true, Juanma."

She leaned closer and whispered into his ear.

"First you went into town, to the market... "

"Alright, well..."

Keeping his voice low so that no one else might overhear him, Juanma recounted what had happened the day before.

"I took the olives to the market. Maria bought all ten kilos, and she gave me a very good price because she said the tourists are here now for Easter, and apparently she can charge them extra."

"And? Then?"

"Well, then I went to the Caleta to have a glass of wine. And like always I tied the mule up in the little field behind the bar so she could graze. Then I went inside. Everyone was there: Fali, Paco, Juan Dios, Antonio and old Jose. Also there were a couple of Americans at the end of the bar drinking whiskey."

"And...?"

"And so Manolo brings me my wine. And I'm standing there then, talking to Jose, when I see Vicente pull up in his fancy Mercedes car. Well, I didn't think anything of it, though I had never seen him at the Caleta before. When he drinks he usually goes to the Gaviota."

"Then what? Don't stop!"

"Okay. So then Vicente walks in..."

"...and he says..."

"...and he says hello to everyone, naturally."

"Naturally."

"And then, Concha, *he walks straight over to me!*"

"My God!"

"He puts his hand on my shoulder. And he says, 'Juanma, I saw your mule outside, and so I stopped because there is something I need to talk to you about.' So I say, 'Okay, what is it you want to talk about?' But then, Concha, he leans toward me very close, like you are now, and he says, 'What I want to talk to you about is very important. So Juanma, if you don't mind I would like to talk to you in private.'"

Concha burst out laughing. She swung around into the chair closest to Juanma and stared at him.

"Keep going! For God's sake, keep going! And then...?"

"Well, then I told Manolo to bring Vicente a glass of wine. And when the wine came he and I, we took our glasses outside and sat at one of the tables in the front.

We were the only ones out there, and I'm thinking to myself, 'Now what could be so important that Vicente Garcia, of all people, wants to talk to *me* in private?' And then, Chita, suddenly I remember he's building that new restaurant in the town. And so I thought, 'Ah ha! Maybe *that's* it. Probably he wants to buy our olives and our almonds for his restaurant, for less than he would have to pay at the market.'"

"Juanma, how silly you are!"

"But then he looks at me very seriously, so seriously, and he says quietly, as if what he's going to say is like some big secret, 'Juanma, I have wanted to talk to you now for a long time. But,' he says, 'I have been very busy. As soon as I could though I was planning to go out to your *cortijo* to talk to you, and to your Papa and to Concha.' Well, then Chita I knew he wanted to talk about more than just olives and almonds."

Concha closed her eyes and took a long deep breath.

"And so then he says, 'Juanma, you and I, we have never talked about this before, but I know that from your land you have a clear view of the urbanization my company is building on the Punta de la Mona. You can see all the houses and apartments going up. Now,' he says, 'I want to tell you something. It will be another year before we are through building, and already, can you believe it, almost every one of those apartments and those houses have been sold."

"Incredible!"

"'The area is changing, Juanma, and changing quickly,' he tells me. 'You probably understand it better than most, because after all you can see those changes from your own house. Tell me,' he asks, 'for how long has your family lived on that *cortijo?*' I tell him, 'Since my father's grandfather was a young man.' So then he says, 'For about a hundred years. That's a long time.' 'Yes,' I say, 'a hundred years is a long time.'"

Juanma took a slow sip from his coffee, then continued.

"He knows, everyone knows, that Papa and his brother fought on the side of the Republicans during the war. And so he says to me 'Your father must be a very clever man to have held onto the *cortijo* after the Nationalists won.' I said, 'Yes, Papa is a clever man.' Then I told him to get to his point, and he laughed and said I must be a clever man, too. Can you imagine, Chita? Vicente Garcia told me I must be a clever man. He told me I would make a good businessman. And so I ask him,

'Okay, what kind of business do you have in mind?'

'On one side of you, Juanma,' he said, 'they are building the new area of Cotobro. While in front of you, we are building our urbanization. So you and your family can see, I think, that not only is our coast changing, but the whole world is changing. We must change with it, Juanma, or we will be left behind. That is why,' he said, 'I am in the business of helping make these changes. I build houses and apartments and restaurants and shops, everything I can, for all these foreigners and rich Spaniards who are coming here. These people are good for us,' he told me, 'because they bring money, and with that money of course jobs.'"

"It's true! He's right. He knows what he's talking about."

"'Today,' he tells me, 'most of the people who want work can find work. And everyone has enough to eat. And what's more, people don't have to work fifteen hour days like they did when your father was a boy. They only work eight hour days now, and *still* have enough to feed their families good. Their children have good schools. And it promises to get *even* better. In other words I'm telling you,' he said, 'the more tourists we can bring here, the more money we will have. And the more money we have, the better it is for everyone.'

"'Now,' he says, 'you asked me to get to my point. The point is, I would like to bring more people here, but I have nowhere to put them. There is only one direction left now that I can build in. "

"And so...?"

"And so then he says to me, 'Juanma, I would like to buy your *cortijo*.'"

Concha stood up. She walked in a great circle around the table.

"*Then* what did he say?"

"Well, then he says, 'Before you tell me anything, Juanma, I want to say that you and I, we have known each other since we were boys. And because of this, I do not want to play some kind of game. Your property is valuable. *Very* valuable. And I refuse to try and convince you otherwise. Though it is true,' he said, 'that much of it is on steep hill. So of course we would have to dynamite a lot, which costs money. A *lot* of money. But,' he told me, 'you have over six hectares, and on that we can build a lot of homes.'"

"How many? Did he say?"

"He didn't say. Who knows? Ten, maybe? Twenty? Maybe more. I don't know. Anyway, 'There is a lot of money involved,' he told me, 'and for this reason, like I said, I don't want to play games. I don't want to make you one offer that you, Juanma, because you have such a good head for business, would try to raise.'"

"Good for you!" cried Concha. "He knows how smart you are! I am *so* proud of you!"

She rushed to her husband and took his chin in her hand. He looked up at her and smiled. She leaned down and kissed him. A long, deep kiss.

"Now go on. Finish the story."

"Maybe we go back to bed first?"

"Are you crazy? Finish the story."

"Okay. So he said, 'I am going to make you an offer that is very generous, and that is absolutely firm. Also, I don't want an answer right away, even if the answer is yes.' Can you imagine, Chita? He's a kind man I think. He has a good heart."

"I think so too. I don't care what people say. He's a good man."

"'So,' he said, 'you must think about it, and talk it over with your family. With Concha, and also with your Papa. I have checked, and the land is registered in your father's name, and so of course you will need his approval. But we've already said your father is a clever man, so I think he will approve my offer which is...'"

Juanma paused for dramatic effect.

"Say it! *Say it, for God's sake!*"

"'...which is fifteen million pesetas.'"

In 1985, fifteen million pesetas was equal to about eighty thousand U.S. dollars.

There was silence for a moment. Finally Concha spoke.

"No. I can't believe it. I just can't. Not until I see that money. *Fifteen million pesetas?* Are you sure that's what he said?"

"I'm sure."

"And you said he's coming here in two days to hear our answer?"

"He said a couple of days."

"Oh, Juanma, I can't wait to tell Papa! Come on! Let's go find him and tell him now."

"Concha..."

"And then I think you and Papa should go straight into town, tell Vicente yes, and sign the papers right away. Before he has a chance to change his mind."

"He won't change his mind, Chita. He's been thinking about this for a long time."

"Come on. Please, Juanma! Let's go tell Papa."

Concha reached for her husband's hand to pull him toward the door. He resisted.

"Not yet. We'll tell him later. Tonight maybe, after Jorge goes to bed."

"But why wait? Why not just tell him now?"

"Because I...I haven't decided how to tell him."

"What do you mean? You just tell him!"

"It's not that simple."

Juanma stared into his coffee.

"I'm not so sure he's going to like this idea."

"Juanma, look at me! *Fifteen million pesetas!* That's more money than Papa, or you or I have ever *dreamed* of having. Well, isn't it?"

"It's not the money."

"What is it, then?"

"The life. It's the life."

"I don't understand."

"This life, it's all he knows. I'm just afraid a change now is going to frighten him."

"Oh, but you're wrong, Juanma. He *will* like the idea. I *know* he will. He is smart, your Papa. Very smart, like we said. And he will see that this is the best thing for all of us. *Especially* for him."

"What are you talking about?"

"Look, he's growing old now. And he has worked so hard all his life. Don't you see? This will mean he won't have to work so hard anymore. Finally, after all these years, he can take a little rest, like he deserves. Oh, Juanma, when I was looking out our window last night, when I couldn't sleep because I was so excited, I pictured what it will be like for you, for me, for Jorge, and for Papa. Can I tell you?"

"Yes. Tell me. Tell me what it will be like."

As Concha spoke, Juanma watched her. She looked beautiful. Eyes sparkling, cheeks glowing. That smile.

"First," she said, "we will buy a big white house! With lots of rooms, and in the middle of the town. Papa and Jorge will each have their own room. Jorge is getting older quickly, Juanma, and soon I think his privacy will be important to him."

Concha reached over and took her husband's hand.

"Maybe we can even buy a house with a balcony. And in the evenings, we can sit out on our balcony and watch the people. Think of it, Juanma. Just think. Also, we will be near the church. That means that Papa, why he can just walk to the church anytime he wants. Morning, afternoon, night...whenever! Can you imagine? Do you know how much that will mean to him?"

Juanma smiled.

"And in the mornings, during the week Jorge will be able to walk to school together with the friends that he will make. And like we said last night, you and Papa, you two can open a little coffee shop. Imagine! At six o'clock," she laughed, "or seven o'clock, whenever you want, you and he can go to the shop, and then you can sit and talk to each other, and to the old men who will come in to drink their coffee and play their dominoes. If you and Papa want to, you can even play with them. Why not?"

"I guess we could."

"Of *course* you could. And then, after Jorge has left for school, and after you and Papa have gone, I will do our laundry...in a *washing machine*, Juanma. An electric washing machine! And while the machine is washing the clothes, I will do the shopping and the housework. Later, when Jorge comes home from school, his dinner will be waiting for him. And you and Papa can close the shop for a few hours, come home too, and we will all eat together. Just like we do always."

"It sounds good, Chita. Really, it sounds good."

"After dinner then, Jorge will go back to school,

Papa will take his siesta, and I will finish the housework. Then, at the end of the day, Jorge will come home and then he can go out to play with his friends. He will have *friends,* Juanma! His own age. Also, if he wants, he can spend some time with Papa. They can even come visit you in the coffee shop. So you see, even work will not be like work anymore. We will have time, all of us, to do what we *want* to do, not just what we *must* do. Can you imagine? And then finally, after you have closed the shop at night, you will come home and we will all be together until Papa and Jorge go to bed. Then you and I, we will have a little time together...alone."

She smiled. Juanma pretended not to understand.

"What do you mean?"

Concha stood up and came to him. Pushing aside her long skirt, she straddled her husband's lap and lay her arms around his neck. She hugged him, looked at him, kissed him, and broke out laughing. But then too excited to stay sitting, she stood and began once again to pace around the room.

"We will have a *television* set, Juanma! Maybe even a color one! And some nights, when we are all together, we will watch our television. Also, we will have friends who will come to our house to visit us, and sometimes we will visit our friends in their houses. But every night, before we go to sleep, we will sit out on our balcony and watch the people."

"You make it sound so...wonderful."

"Oh, it *will* be! And Papa *will* like the idea, Juanma. I *know* he will. I can't wait to see the look on his face when we tell him."

Juanma finished his coffee and stood.

"We'll talk about it more later."

He started toward the door. Concha rushed after him.

"He *will* like it," she said again, pressing against his chest and closing her eyes. "Don't worry Juanma. Believe me, he will see that it is for the best."

Juanma kissed her on the forehead, then headed out the door.

The sun was quite high in the sky already, and in the bright light Juanma could see his father and his son picking mushrooms and gathering snails in the little field below the house. He stood there for a while watching them. Then he turned and headed up the pathway to the barn.

He was a tall man, and had to stoop low in order to get through the door. Inside it was cool and dark and smelled of time. It took a moment for his eyes to focus.

Once they had, he made his way toward the back, stepping over coiled ropes and sacks of lime and old half-rusted tools that were no longer any good, but that neither he nor his father had ever even thought of throwing out. Here and there a small hole in the tile roof let in a shaft of light, and as he walked a cloud of dust rose from the floor and flies buzzed and the mule snorted.

Above the mule's stall, hanging on the wall, was a rope. Juanma took it down and wrapped it around the mule's neck. Then he swung open the large wooden door at the back of the stall. A mass of bright light came flooding in. Juanma's eyes squinted as he led the mule outside.

He led the mule down the pathway, past the old wall and along the edge of the vineyard until they came to the olive grove. There they turned, wending through rows of trees until they came to a small field. Red poppies were bending in a breeze coming off the sea. Juanma led the mule into the middle of the field. He drove a wooden stake into the ground, tied the rope to the stake and left the mule to graze.

Back inside the barn, he pulled a pair of canvas gloves out of an old tin and shook them hard to make sure there were no spiders lurking in the fingers. Then he grabbed a handsaw and headed back down to the olive grove. He had been pruning the olive trees for almost two weeks already and was nearing the end of the last row. If they were going to sell the *cortijo,* it meant these trees would probably be cut down to make room for whatever Vicente planned to build. Still, Juanma liked to finish what he had started. So picking up where he had left off before the rains had come, he climbed a wooden ladder that was leaning against one tree, and began to cut away the oldest branches.

Olive trees bear their fruit best on younger branches. After a while the branch will still bear fruit, only less and less each year until finally an old branch will take more from the tree than it will give. By cutting the old branches away each spring, room was made to accommodate new growth. And now as Juanma cut the old branches fell in scattered piles on the ground.

Back inside the house, Concha was sitting at the kitchen table writing out a list of the things she needed to do that day. She was also writing down each item that the family would be having for dinner.

Concha was the only one in the family who knew how to read and write, and since marrying Juanma and moving onto the *cortijo* she had gotten into the habit of making long detailed lists of everything from chores to menus. It was her only chance to write, and she was afraid that unless she practiced every day it was a skill she would forget.

Concha had never been out of the area. Nor had anyone she knew. That meant that there was no one with whom she could have corresponded. Years before, when she was a young girl, she had written some poetry now and then. But there was no longer time for that. From the moment she woke to the moment she went to bed her days were busy working. Aside from Sunday mornings, when at Aurelio's urging she would read a few pages of the Bible to the family, her only real chance to use printed words were at moments like this. Sometimes, if there was a little extra money, Juanma would bring her a magazine from town. When he did that she would sit up at night after everyone else had gone to bed and read every word, including the advertisements.

Concha's father had been a fisherman, her mother a fisherman's wife. Though they were poor, the family had had what it needed to survive. No less, no more. Concha and her two brothers grew up in one of what

used to be the many huts built by fishermen along the local beaches. One of the fondest memories she had of that childhood was of one of her mother's cousins, whom Concha called Aunt Carmen. Aunt Carmen knew how to read and write. Whenever she would visit, she would gather the children into one corner of the hut and read to them. Concha always made a point of looking over her shoulder while she read, and it was in that way that she herself learned how to read. When Carmen died, she left behind instructions that her Bible be left to Concha. It was the only book Concha had ever owned, and it had occurred to her that if the family was indeed going to soon have some money, then other books, for her and also for Jorge, would be among the first things she would buy.

As usual, the first item on Concha's list read "Wash dishes." When she was through writing, she gathered the morning dishes that were still scattered about the table, put them into a large bucket and carried them outside.

There was no running water inside the house. Rather, outside the kitchen, beyond the edge of the broken stone patio, was a series of three concrete troughs, or pools. Fresh water from a natural spring ran into the uppermost of these. When that was full, the water spilt over into a second pool. The first pool was the source of the family's drinking water. Every two or three days Concha would fill two five-liter cans and carry them into the kitchen. The second pool was where she washed the family's clothes and dishes. A third pool was where the animals were led each evening to drink.

Concha rested the bucket of dishes on the ground, rolled the sleeves of her dress up above her elbows and began to wash the dishes. A big oak tree provided cool shade over the water. A bird was singing in its branches, and as she scrubbed Concha also began to sing. As far as she knew she had everything in the world to look forward to, and nothing to fear.

Jorge and Aurelio had by now gathered all of the mushrooms and the snails they were able to find in the field below the house, and were heading to the vineyard.

"That last snail was pretty fast," said the old man. "Good thing you caught him."

"He wasn't so fast, Abuelito."

"No?"

"No."

Aurelio stopped to take off his hat and wipe the

sweat from his face. As he did, Jorge tugged on one of his trouser legs.

"Abuelito?"

"Yes, my little one?"

"When are you going to teach me how to whitewash?"

The old man laughed.

"Just as soon as the last of the almonds are shelled."

"When will that be?"

"Not to worry. In a few moments we will take these snails and these mushrooms to your mother. Then we will finish with the almonds. And then, after we have eaten and taken our siestas, I am going to... "

"I know!" shouted the boy. "Then you are going to teach me how to make our house and our barn even more beautiful than they already are!"

"That's right."

"Abuelito?"

"Yes?"

"I wish it was afternoon already."

The old man looked down at his grandson.

"No," he said quietly. "You must never wish that. You must never wish that the future should come early. One day you will understand," he said, "that the future, it will be here soon enough. And once it is, my little one, the past will be gone forever."

When she was through washing and drying the dishes, Concha brought them inside and put them on shelves fashioned from old wooden fruit crates. Then she crossed to a nearby closet, pulled out a homemade broom and started to sweep the floors. She finished with the kitchen and was beginning her and Juanma's room when the broom started to fall apart. Usually she would make a new broom with the leaves of palma plants that grew beside the house. But now she burst out laughing. Soon, it occurred to her, once they were living in the town, she would simply walk into a store, put some money on the counter and buy herself a ready-made broom, one that would last not weeks, but possibly years. Life was about to get so much easier!

She managed to finish sweeping by bending over and holding the loose leaves together with her hand. When she was finished, she walked to the kitchen table, took her pencil and wrote at the bottom of her list, "Make broom." Then she gathered a basket full of dirty laundry from Jorge's and Aurelio's room and carried it outside to the spring.

Concha's hair was tied into a loose bun. A few

wisps fell around her face as she began to work each piece of clothing against an old washboard. While she scrubbed, she again sang to herself.

Jorge and Aurelio, now finished with their work in the vineyard, carried the snails and mushrooms into the kitchen. Aurelio tied a knot in the plastic bag so the snails could not escape, then he left the bag on the kitchen table for Concha. He took Jorge's little hand in his and together they went back outside. They made their way around the house to a far comer of the patio. From there they had a clear view of the sea and the Punta in the distance, and Vicente's crew hard at work.

There were grapes growing above that comer of the patio. The vines clung to wires that Aurelio had strung many years before. The new leaves were big and green and there was shade under them. A lemon tree grew nearby, and there was also a prickly pear cactus.

At the center of the patio there were two dead olive tree stumps standing next to each other. Behind each stump was a battered cane chair. On the cement ground between the chairs, covered with a sheet of plastic to protect them from the recent rain, was an empty basket and a burlap sack. The bottom of the sack held some unshelled almonds.

Aurelio let go of Jorge's hand, then sat behind the taller of the two stumps. He spread his legs out on either side of the dead wood, bent down and rolled the sheet of plastic into a bundle that he laid to one side. Then he fished two small iron bars out of the burlap sack and placed one on top of each stump. Alongside them he piled a handful of unshelled almonds.

Jorge hopped onto the chair next to his grandfather's. He watched as Aurelio picked up his iron bar and began to crack the almonds open. Jorge tried to do the same, but his little hand had a hard time holding onto the almonds as he struck them. It took him half a dozen tries or so to expose each nut, while the old man cracked each almond with a single stroke in a smooth, steady rhythm.

Concha finished washing the clothes, and was hanging them to dry on a clothesline that stretched from one corner of the house.

"Concha," Aurelio shouted out, "do you sing for joy, or to drive your grief away?"

"I sing for joy!" she shouted back.

The old man looked at Jorge.

"Your mother seems to be in a fine mood today."

"That," said Jorge without looking up, "is because she knows how much we love her."

When Concha was finished, she went back to the kitchen, sat down at the table and crossed "Laundry" off her list. Then she gave some more thought to the menu for the midday meal. Dinner, she had decided, was going to be something special, a feast over which to celebrate the good news. She could not wait for her husband to decide to tell his father. And in her excitement, she was even forgetting that it was a Friday. And not just any Friday. This was Good Friday, before Easter.

Some months earlier the family had butchered a pig. It was hanging, parts salted, others smoked, in the little cellar under the kitchen. Concha wrote the word "Meat." Then next on her list she wrote "Garlic soup." That was the old man's favorite. She smiled thinking how delighted he would be. Then she wrote "Bake bread." Finally, she made a list of the vegetables she would gather from the garden. "Tomatoes," "Cucumbers," "Red peppers," "Fava beans." When the list was finished she grabbed a straw basket from under the counter and headed to the garden.

After she'd picked what she needed, she left the basket in the kitchen and headed up the pathway to a spot beyond the old wall. There she gathered the bottom of her skirt into her hand so as not to trip over it, and scrambled over some rocks, then up the hill until she came to the three terraced rows of trees. Using her apron as a pouch, she gathered avocados and blood-oranges until she had as many as she needed, then carried those back to the house. On her way down she also stopped to collect some eggs from the chicken coop, and a small bouquet of yellow daisies that she would place on the table.

Back inside the house, she struck a match and lit a lantern that hung from the ceiling in the center of the room. Carrying the lantern in one hand, and a sharp knife in the other, she pulled aside a faded yellow curtain and slowly made her way down a narrow flight of stone steps that led into the little cellar.

There were a few pigeons and a rabbit hanging from a wooden beam at the bottom of the stairs. She had to push past those to get to where the pig was hanging. Holding the flame high so that she could see, Concha squeezed between slabs of meat, pushing them aside until she found what she was looking for. Then she placed the lantern onto the dirt floor. With the light from the fire flickering against the blade, she reached up and proceeded to cut out what she needed.

It was cool in the cellar. Not just now in the spring, but even in the height of summers, which made it ideal for keeping meat. Also for storing wine. Dusty bottles of the old man's *vino del terreno* were stacked against one wall. Concha grabbed one of these as she headed back up to the kitchen.

Near the mouth of the stairs were four large clay jars. The first held vinegar that Concha made each fall using some of their wine. The second and third jars contained olives soaking in a brine of seawater, vinegar and fresh herbs. The fourth jar contained olive oil that Juanma had pressed from their own olives.

Standing in the kitchen, Concha wiped the meat clean with a damp cloth, smeared it with some of the

olive oil, and pressed some cloves of fresh garlic into the meat. Then she laid some rosemary on top of it, covered it with a cloth and went outside to start the fire. The others would think the fire was only for baking the day's bread. She wanted the meat to be a surprise.

Concha did all her baking and cooking in the adobe oven behind the house. The oven was shaped like a dome and divided into three chambers. The largest on the bottom was for the fire. Above this were the ovens. The chamber on the left had a brick bottom, sealing it off from the fire. That was used for baking bread. The other chamber had a metal grate below it, exposing it to the open flames. That one was used for roasting meats and vegetables.

Nearby there was a small shed in which the firewood was kept. The dirt floor was littered with thick piles of old almond husks. Concha scooped up a handful of these and carried them to the oven. Using the husks as kindling she quickly got a fire started. Once the flames had taken hold she went back into the kitchen.

Jorge, meanwhile, had finished shelling his little pile of almonds.

"You see, Abuelito?" he said proudly, holding them up. "I can do them almost as fast as you can!"

Aurelio was about to say something when there was an explosion in the distance. It was followed in rapid succession by another, and then still another. They came so quickly and were so loud that they frightened Jorge and made him jolt. His handful of almonds fell to the ground. The old man looked out over the patio in the direction of the Punta. A cloud of smoke and dust was rising above the area they had just dynamited.

"Why are they doing that, Abuelito?"

"Because...because they do not like the hill the way it is. So they use dynamite to make it the way that they want it."

"Is it good that they do that?"

The old man thought about it for a moment.

"No, it is not good. But it is not bad either. It just is, that's all."

Jorge nodded like he understood. He looked toward the Punta as he felt the old man's arm reach around his shoulder. Jorge thought that it was meant to comfort him, and he was about to tell his grandfather that it was all right, he was not afraid, but when he looked up he realized that it was Aurelio who needed comforting. For the first time in his life, Jorge saw his grandfather cry.

Sometimes, when looking at a piece of wood, or the side of a hill, or even the stars at night, in one's imagination one can see the features of a face. After doing so it can be hard, almost impossible, to look at that

wood or that hill or those stars without seeing that face. So it was with Aurelio. When he had been a boy, his father had pointed out to him on the side of the Punta the smiling face of a man. He had two caves for eyes, a large rock for a nose, and a long narrow crevice for a mouth. Now though, when the smoke finally cleared, Aurelio could see that the man's face was still there, but he was no longer smiling. With the crevice blown and twisted into a different shape, it looked like he was in pain.

Back inside the kitchen, Concha was putting the fava beans and red peppers into a pan together with the mushrooms Jorge and Aurelio had picked that morning. In a moment they would be added to the fire. The bread was already in the oven. So, too, were the meat and potatoes. Now she turned to preparing the garlic soup, and an avocado and blood-orange salad she would serve as desert.

Everything was done except the setting of the table, and for that Concha had something very special in mind.

She left the kitchen and went into her and Juanma's bedroom. In the bottom drawer of a battered old chest she kept her most prized possessions. There was the silk scarf Juanma had bought her just before they were married. There was the white sweater she had made herself some years before, that she wore the few times each year when the family went to church. There was the Bible from her Aunt Carmen, of course, and a gold wedding band that had also been Carmen's. Concha was saving that to give to Jorge one day, so that he would have it to give to his own bride. And there were some old half-faded photos of her family. One of her father on the beach in La Herradura, standing alongside the little boat in which he was last seen. And another of her parents together with all three children, taken when Concha was about four years old. There was a photo of herself and Juanma on their wedding day. She stared at that one for a long time. How happy they looked! She smiled, realizing she was just as happy now, because once again the future seemed so full of possibility.

Carefully, she laid the photos back into the drawer, then pulled out a white linen tablecloth that had been her mother's. Her mother had embroidered a string of yellow daisies along the edges. Concha had been thinking of them when she picked the yellow daisies from beside the stone wall.

Clutching the cloth to her chest, Concha went back into the kitchen. Using a damp towel, she carefully wiped the wooden table until she was absolutely sure that it was clean. Then she unfurled her mother's tablecloth and spread it out across the table. It had been lying in the drawer since Christmas, and where it had been folded there were creases. Using her hands, Concha rubbed the tablecloth as smooth as she could. And as she did, suddenly she began to cry.

Her mother had spent a long hard life as the wife of a poor fisherman. She had died a lonely widow, with almost nothing to her name. Now that Concha for the first time in her life was about to have some real money, there were so many things she wished that she could do for her mother. But that wasn't meant to be. Instead, she would do everything she could for Jorge. That would also please her mother.

Through the kitchen window a breeze was blowing. Concha could hear Jorge and Aurelio cracking open the last of the almonds. She finished setting the table, then went outside to check on the bread and the meat. Juanma had finished pruning the olive trees and was dragging the thickest branches toward the barn. Later in the day when the air was cooler he would begin cutting them into firewood.

Finally everything was ready. Concha stood back to take a last look at the table. The family only had one set of dishes, yet somehow they managed to look special laid out on her mother's tablecloth. In the middle of the table in an old glass jar she had put the yellow daisies.

She stepped outside to call to everyone to come in.

"Mama, look!" Jorge cried. His little eyes were smiling.

Aurelio had tossed all of the almonds he had shelled into the basket on the ground. Jorge had been keeping his in a separate pile, and now he proudly showed them to his mother.

"You see how many I did?" he askd. "Almost as many as Abuelito."

"And next year," the old man added, "when your hands are bigger, you will do more than me. And twice as fast, I'm sure of it."

"I can see you've both been working very hard. You must be very hungry. Come on now, both of you, food is on the table."

"Mama?"

"Yes?"

"Do you know what we will do after we eat?"

"What will you do?"

"Abuelito and I, we are going to make our house and our barn even more beautiful than they are already."

"That's right," said the old man. "That is *exactly* what we are going to do."

"Come on, you two. Before it gets cold."

Aurelio and Jorge headed up to the pools to wash their hands. The water was cool. The fire in the oven was still burning, and the old man shouted through the open window of the kitchen.

"Concha, what is it you are cooking that smells so good?"

"It's a surprise!" she yelled back. "Come and see for yourself!"

Jorge had run in and was already seated at the table when Aurelio appeared in the doorway. At the sight of the table he froze.

"But...what's all this?" he asked.

"Sit down, Papa. Please," Concha blurted out. "Juanma will explain it all to you in minute."

The old man kept standing in the doorway, just staring at the table.

"But, what day is this? It's not Sunday yet, is it?

Not Easter?" He was confused. "Isn't today Friday?"

"Yes, Papa."

"But... "

"Please sit down. Like I said, Juanma will explain everything to you."

She took his hand and led him to his seat.

All the old man could think of as he looked around was that they were in the middle of the Holy Week. They were supposed to be fasting, not feasting.

Juanma walked into the kitchen. Like his father, he also froze when he saw the table. He shot a quick glance at Concha.

"Please, Juanma, sit down."

Without saying a word, Juanma sat across the table from his father.

"Will somebody please tell me what's going on?" asked the old man.

"Good news!" Concha cried out. She could not contain her excitement any longer. "Some *very* good news!"

A BITTER FEAST

"Garlic soup!" Aurelio cried, noticing the bowl in front of him. "My favorite. But... we'll have this on Sunday, won't we? For our Easter dinner?"

"Yes," said Concha, grinning. "Twice this week, just for you!" She leaned over to stroke his hand. The old man was more confused by the minute.

"And, what's this? You've made a roast!" he blurted out, seeing the meat steaming on the counter. He looked over at his son.

"Juanma? What's going on?"

Juanma had not known about Concha's plan to

prepare such a feast. He had not expected to have to reveal Vicente's offer to his father quite so soon. Though he had realized while working in the trees it was not fair to Concha to put it off much longer. What's more, like his father he felt uneasy having such a meal on this of all days. They never ate meat on a Friday. And this was not just any Friday. It was the Friday before Easter. His father, like his mother when she was alive, believed strongly in their church and its dictates. If he had known of Concha's plan, Juanma would have tried to stop her. Still, he could understand her excitement. And they had to tell his father sooner or later. It's just that he would have found another way of doing it. If only he had not delayed the news out of fear.

"Let's start the soup, eh Papa?" he said, trying to buy time to collect his thoughts.

On the table was an old tureen, its edges chipped and cracked. Concha eagerly poured a ladle full of garlic soup from it into the old man's bowl. There was already a raw egg at the bottom of his bowl, and as she poured Concha whipped the soup with a fork so that the raw egg swirled up into the hot broth where it cooked immediately. She did the same for Juanma and Jorge and herself. Then she sat, and the family joined hands.

As before every meal, Aurelio said the grace. Usually he only said a few words. Thank you for this, Lord, thank you for that... But today he chose to say the Lord's Prayer, every word, reciting each line slowly and thoughtfully. As he spoke, Concha worried that the soup would get cold. When he finally finished she was the first to say "Amen."

The bread was still warm from the oven. The old man took it from its basket and sliced it. Everyone took a piece.

The bottle of wine Concha had taken from the cellar stood open on the table. She filled each of their glasses, then lifted hers.

"A toast," she said. "To the future!"

Jorge had been given a sip's worth of wine in his own little glass.

"Mama, are we celebrating something?"

Suddenly the old man's face broke into a smile. It had just occurred to him what all this fuss was about. Surely, Juanma and Concha were about to announce that they were expecting a second child.

Now it made sense! *That* was why Concha had been singing all morning! And in her excitement, she must have just forgotten that it was Friday. Of course!

That was understandable. And forgivable. It was so obvious. Concha had been to town a week earlier to buy provisions. She could easily have seen the doctor then. Juanma had been to town the day before, and could have gotten the results. That would explain why he had been acting so strangely since he had come back. Aurelio burst out laughing. There was nothing in the world that could have made him happier.

"My children," he said now, "listen to me. No doubt there is, as you say, good news to celebrate today. But you know something? I was just thinking that really, *everyday* of our lives is good news. So why should we even need some excuse to celebrate, eh? I mean after all, aren't we very lucky? Don't we have each other *everyday?* And a fine home *everyday?* I think, therefore, that we should *celebrate* everyday!"

He seemed drunk with joy, as he took a second sip from his wine. Concha, too, began to laugh.

"What is it we're celebrating, Mama?" asked Jorge.

The old man looked across the table at his son.

"Yes, come on. We can't wait any longer. Jorge and I, we want to know. Tell us, what is the good news?"

Juanma glanced at his wife.

"Well, yesterday, when I went into the town after

I sold the olives at the market..."

"Yes?"

"I went to the Caleta for a glass of wine."

"And?"

"And while I was there, I ran into Vicente Garcia."

Vicente was not the town doctor. He was a real estate broker. The one who was building the urbanization on the Punta.

"And? So? What does Vicente Garcia have to do with us?"

Juanma cleared his throat and looked his father in the eye.

"Papa, Vicente would like to buy our *cortijo*."

A moment passed. Then another. Aurelio said nothing. He did not move. He just sat there staring across the table at his son.

"Papa?"

Silence.

"Papa?" asked Concha. "Did you hear?"

"I heard."

Concha reached over and again put her hand on the old man's arm.

"Isn't it wonderful, Papa? He has offered us fifteen million pesetas. Can you imagine? Fifteen million!"

Aurelio's eyes remained fixed on Juanma's. He still had a sort of half-smile on his face. As if frozen there from before. Finally, he spoke.

"*This* is the good news we are celebrating?"

"Yes, Papa. Isn't it wonderful?"

The old man nodded. "Wonderful. And you, Juanma? Do you also think this is so wonderful?"

Juanma could feel his father's eyes boring into him.

"I do, Papa. Yes. And please, let me tell you why. Because, whatever we decide to do, if we decide to sell to him or not, it is I think the first time in our lives we have a real choice to make. Before," he continued, "there was only one choice really. Work all day six days a week here on the *cortijo.* Or go hungry. But now, Papa, suddenly we have a real choice. And yes, that I think is wonderful."

Father and son sat staring at each other. Concha watched them. It looked like they were both carved out of stone. The same stone.

Juanma for his part could not think clearly with his father staring at him like that. He wanted to say something to end the silence, but he couldn't think of anything. What he said about having a choice had come to him earlier while he was working in the olive trees.

He had hoped then that everything that followed would come naturally, and easily. He could see now from his father's face that it was going to be anything but easy.

Jorge was the only one eating. For a while the only sound at the table came from his spoon scraping the bottom of his bowl. Then Concha suddenly began to laugh again. But now it was a nervous laugh instead of the happy laugh it was before.

"Papa, fifteen million pesetas is a lot of money. More money than any of us has ever even dreamed of having. Why, it's a small fortune!"

"And what," Aurelio asked, turning to look at her, "what is it you would like to buy with this small fortune?"

"A house, Papa!" she answered immediately. "In the town. One with many rooms, so that you and Jorge could each have your own room."

Jorge looked up.

"Mama, are we going to sell our *cortijo?*"

"We're just talking about it."

"And we could get a little coffee shop," Juanma jumped in, "where you and I, Papa, we could work together just like we do here. But the work would be much easier, and the hours shorter."

"So we would have more time to spend together as a family," added Concha. "You have worked so hard, Papa, for so many years now. You deserve something better."

Slowly, a real smile reappeared on the old man's face.

"My children, bless you. *Bless you!* For I can see now, even with these old eyes, why it is you want to do this. That you would give up all of this," he said, waving his hand as if pointing to the whole *cortijo*, "for me, means more to me than I can ever tell you. But listen, I will tell you something. I do not mind the work. In fact, the truth is that I love it. I shouldn't say so, because now you will expect me to do even more. But it's true. Even if I do complain sometimes that my back is tired, or my feet are sore. And what's more, as for having my own room, well the truth is I would miss Jorge. For we two make a couple of fine roommates, don't we?"

Jorge's mouth was full. He nodded.

"There! You see!" Aurelio laughed. "So you worry about nothing. These things you mention, they are not problems. They are blessings."

He reached over to take Concha's hand.

"Still," he said, "you two, both of you, are being

kind. Very kind. And you must not think I do not appreciate it, because I do. Really. But you must never think of selling your home, our home, for my sake. So, enough talk about that, eh? Now then, Concha, let's eat this fine meal you've made for us."

Concha and Juanma looked at each other.

"Papa," said Concha, "it's not only you that we are worried about. It is also Jorge."

"I don't understand."

"What I mean is that next year Jorge will start to go to school. When you were a boy, Papa, and also when Juanma was a boy, you two did not have to go to school. No one said anything about it. But today it's different. There's a law now, and it's a good law. Children must go to school. So whether we are living here, or in the town, Jorge will have to go to school."

"Okay, so he'll go to school. He can walk. The town is not so far. It will be good for him."

"Papa, for school he is going to need new clothes, and books. And those things cost money. A lot of money."

"Well now look, if it is money you two are worried about, that I can understand. So let me tell you something. Something I have been keeping a secret for a long time, but I can see now that it is time for you to know. It happens that I have put a little something away. Something that, if you should ever need it, is for you to use. You will find, sewn into the foot of the mattress on my bed, ninety thousand pesetas."

It was the equivalent of about five hundred U.S. dollars.

"I have been saving it," he went on, "so that I would never become a burden to you. And now that you know it is there, well, you two shouldn't have to worry about money any more. Agreed? Your son will have all of the clothes, and all of the books, he needs!"

"Papa," said Concha, "ninety thousand pesetas...a long time ago, that was a lot of money. But today, it isn't."

"Alright then," said Aurelio, frustrated. "If it's even more than that you need, Concha. If ninety thousand pesetas, as you say, is not enough, well still that does not mean we have to sell our home. There are other things we can do."

"Like?"

"Well, like above the orange trees, for instance, there is room to plant three more rows of avocados. Mind you, avocados get a good price at the market. A *very* good price. It would mean a little extra work, yes, but then it would also mean a lot more money. And besides," he looked at Jorge, "Jorge is getting older quickly, and is already helping more and more. We could do it. And if you need even more money than that, why we could raise two pigs a year instead of just one. And we could sell the second pig to your friend Vicente Garcia!" He laughed. "So you see, Concha, money is not the problem. That you two worry too much, that is the problem."

The old man was still holding onto Concha's hand, and smiling.

"It's not just the money," Concha answered. "If we are living here, Papa, when Jorge begins his school, then that will mean he will have to walk two kilometers every morning to get to town. And then another two kilometers home again. He can do it, yes, but I ask you, how much time will that leave him to do his homework? Not much. Not enough. Especially if, like you say, he will also have to help with more of the chores around here. But," she added, "if we are living in the town, well then the school will be nearby. He will not have to walk all that way. Instead, he could spend that time studying. Don't you see, Papa, how that way he would be a better student?"

"A better student of what?" Aurelio asked. "How, for instance, is he going to learn how to run a farm if we are living in the town?"

"Papa," said Concha, "if we sell the *cortijo*, then that is something he would not need to learn."

The old man now let go of Concha's hand.

"This is our home," he said, "yet you talk about it like it was a basket full of olives to be sold at market."

"Papa... "

"I did not know that you, either of you, thought this way. Tell me, *why*? Our life here is good, isn't it?"

He was looking at Juanma when he asked this, but it was Concha who shot back with the answer.

"Yes, Papa," she said, "but the life in town is even better."

Aurelio's breathing became heavier.

"Let me tell you something," he said. "This life here was good enough for my father, and for his father before him. It has been good enough for me. And I thought, Juanma, that it has been good for you, also."

"Yes, Papa. It has been good. *Very* good. Only... "

"Only what?"

"It's just that…it's not the *only* life."

"Times are changing," Concha said. "Papa, tell

me. How will Jorge be able to live like his grandfather, or his grandfather's father, when all these modern houses and apartments, and hotels and shops, and everything else are being built everywhere around us? Hmm? Just across the water, on the Punta, everyday now you hear the dynamite. You see what they're doing. The whole world is changing, Papa. And if we do not change with it, do you know who's going to be left behind? Not you. Not me, so much. Not Juanma. But *Jorge*! And someday, Jorge's children.

"Listen to me, please," she continued. "It is not like when you were a boy anymore. Or even when Juanma was a boy. Everything is changing *so fast*. Tell me, what do you think it will be like when they are finished building over there and the rich people move in? It's one thing now to watch them building. But it will be very different when they are through."

She reached once again for Aurelio's hand, but he pulled it away.

"It was alright for you to be poor when you were growing up, because all of the people who lived nearby, they were poor also. And like them, you worked hard, you ate, you slept, and that was it. You believed yours was the best life around, and you were right…because it was the *only* life around. You could not see, everyday, other lives even better. Easier. But now look, Papa. That's *all* we can see. There are no more poor neighbors. No other *cortijos*. We're the last."

Concha was growing more and more excited as she spoke.

"On the hill over there," she said, pointing toward the Punta, "he will see children. But they will be rich children, Papa. And Jorge will not want to play with them. Why? Because he will not have fancy toys like they will have. Or nice clothes like they will wear. He will hear music coming from their houses, but he will not have a radio. And at nights, he will even see the lights from their television sets through their windows. And then later, when he sees those same children at school, they will tell him what they have seen on television. And what will Jorge say? What will he tell them? That we do not have a television, because we do not even have *electricity?* They will laugh at him! Think about it, Papa. Think of what it will be like for him."

"I will tell you what it will be like for him," the old man shot back. "Like it was for me when I was growing up. And for Juanma, also, when he was a boy. He will not need a television set, or fancy toys. He will have the sea where he can swim, and trees to climb. A mule to ride, and a family that loves him. I know about these new rich families," Aurelio went on. "The husband is always at work making money. And the mother? She works too, so that they will have more money than anyone could need. And what do the children do? They watch this television you talk so good about. The sea is there, and do they swim in it? No! They swim in swimming pools, like the ones your good friend Vicente is building on the Punta now. Why? Because they think they are too good to swim in the sea together with the dolphins and the fish.

"Such children grow up quickly," he said. "Too quickly! And do you know what is the saddest thing of all? Not once, not once, do they ever hear the sound of silence. They live with noise, noise, always noise. From their cars, and their telephones, and their precious televisions. They live with so much noise, they cannot hear themselves think!

"At night," the old man continued, "they cannot see the stars, because they surround themselves with lights that shroud the stars. And the saddest thing of all? *They do not even know it!* They come out to the country once or twice, and they say 'Oh my, but you have a lot of stars here!' As if they did not have just as many stars above their cities and their towns like we have in the country. The stars are everywhere, for everyone! But they do not see them. You know why? Because the stars are free, and they are interested only in those things that cost money."

Aurelio's eyes flared. He began now to throw his arms about in wild gestures. From across the table,

Juanma watched his father. He looked like a wild animal that had been cornered and was fighting for its life.

"This...this better life you talk about," Aurelio cried, "take a good close look at it! The food they eat, even the wine they drink, it all has chemicals in it. Is *that* what you want for your boy? Hmm, well? Is it?" He pointed at the table. "Look! Do you see what we are eating here? Vegetables from our own garden. Meat we have slaughtered ourselves, and that we know is clean and without chemicals. We drink this wine that we made from our own grapes with *these!*" he shouted, holding up both hands. "It has our sweat, and our blood in it." The old man glanced at the wall above Juanma. Hanging there in an old frame was a faded reproduction of da Vinci's Last Supper.

"Not to mention, *His* blood."

Aurelio took a long deep breath, then continued.

"If Jorge grows up here, yes, he will have to work hard. His hands will get dirty. And no, at the end of the day he will not watch television. But he will go to sleep knowing he has had an honest day, and that he is an honest man who does not steal a living from the world, but who lives simply and is happy with what he has.

"In the town," he added, "it is not honest. The

people there are not honest. They make their money by buying from one person, and then selling to another, to a friend even, for more than they themselves have had to pay for the same thing. With *this* money, then, they buy their cars, and their television sets, and their fancy clothes. And still they want more. More, more, always more! What you are talking about, Concha, is putting sugar in the cake and leaving out the flour!"

Jorge was holding a piece of bread in one hand and his spoon in the other. But even he was not eating. Instead, he was just watching his grandfather. It was the first time he had ever seen the old man so angry, and it frightened him.

"Papa," said Juanma, "much of what you say is true. But don't you see? If we do not go to the town, well then it will only be so long before the town will come to us. Look out the window! Already, it is almost here. Then what will we do, Papa? Build a wall and hide behind it? Pretend that new world is not out there? Hear no evil, see no evil? Should we stay here and just watch while they blast away at the hills all around us, bit by bit, until one night they will have built so many lights that you, *you* Papa, will step outside and from right here, from our own house, you will look up at the sky and not see any stars?

"Or," Juanma asked, "do we leave now, before that happens? Holding our heads high. Using them, like they are determined to use us?"

"That is the way the world works today," Concha added.

"Well then what I say is, fuck the world!"

"*Papa!*"

There was a long silence.

"I'm sorry," the old man said. "Jorge, I'm sorry."

Jorge looked down at the floor, pretending that he hadn't heard that.

"Papa," Juanma pleaded, "listen to me. Please. What you say about our life here, it's true. It *is* clean. It *is* honest. But there is another side to it. Here on the *cortijo* we work, what, twelve hours a day maybe? Six days a week? Even on Sundays we must tend to the animals, and so never do we have a chance to do other things, see other things, or even think about other things. Also, Papa, think about Concha. For just a minute, I beg you. We have one son and no daughter. Here in the country the men, we have our work. And the women, they have theirs. If Jorge is to run this *cortijo* someday, well then he must spend all his time with you and me, to learn what it is we, the men, do. That's fine for us, yes? And if we had a daughter, okay, maybe it would be different. But we don't. At night, Papa, sometimes when we are alone, Concha tells me how she wishes there was another woman she could talk to. You can understand that, can't you?"

"It's true," pleaded Concha. "But even more important, when Jorge is in school, if he has to walk so far everyday, and do his chores, and do his homework, then how much time will he have left to climb those trees you talk about? Or go swimming in the sea?

"If only you knew," she said, fighting back tears, "how badly I want for him to have an education. Something none of us ever had the chance to get. But that he now *does* have a chance to get! Should we deny him that?"

"What are you talking about? You know how to read and write."

"Yes, okay, it's true. But Papa, I don't know *what* to read. Or *what* to write. Everyday," she cried, "I make these stupid little lists of everything I have to do around the house. Is *that* why I learned to write? Well, is it? And those," she pointed to an old stack of magazines in the corner, "are *those* all that I'm supposed to read?"

"You can read the Bible!"

"Yes, you're right. And I do. But what *else* can I read? What else will Jorge read? The Bible is not the *only* book."

Aurelio stared at her. This was too much.

"In the school, Papa, Jorge will read many books. And he will learn many things."

"Mama?"

"Yes?"

"I don't want to read a lot of books. I want to be like Papa and Abuelito."

"*No!*" shouted the old man. "Your mama does not want you to be like us. *You must be better than us!*"

"Not better," Concha cried, "but better educated, yes!" She lowered her voice. "I want that so bad for him. So that someday, when my son becomes a man, he will have a choice *how* he wants to live, and *where* he wants to live. And yes, what he wants to be. Maybe he will *want* to be a farmer. And if that's so, Papa, I promise you, nobody will ever stop him. But," she added, "maybe he will want to be a teacher. Or a doctor. Or maybe even...an astronaut."

"I want to be a farmer, Mama."

"*There! You see?*" declared the old man.

"That's what I mean!" shouted Concha, beside herself. "He is only six years old, and already he says he wants to be a farmer. And *why?* I'll tell you why. *Because that's all he's seen!* How can he know, at six years old, what he wants to be when he is grown-up? When other children at the school are talking about what they want to be, will Jorge say to them 'I will be a farmer, because that's all I can be. It's all I know.'"?

"No!" Aurelio answered. "If we lived in the town, he could not tell them he wanted to be a farmer. Even if that was what he wanted more than anything. Because if he said to them 'When I grow up, I want to be a farmer like my father, and my grandfather, and even my grandfather's father. I want to live by working with my hands in the dirt, to breathe clean air, not city air. Drink fresh water, not this city water that tastes like chemicals.' If he said to them he did not want more than he would need, well then they would *laugh* at him. They would think he was an idiot, and call him stupid. Why? Because everybody thinks country people are stupid people.

"Look at you, Concha. Even you think that, and you are one of us. Have you forgotten already how poor you were when Juanma married you? Hmm?

Well, have you? Your father was a poor fisherman, who had nothing to his name but a little boat, some ropes, some nets, and a shack on the beach that didn't even belong to him. And he paid the price for that with his life. But now," Aurelio said, "now you have land and a real house. Your supper, and your son's supper, they only depend on simple work. No more, no less. If you eat or not, it does not depend on luck, like it did when your father had to fish for the family's dinner. You've told me yourself, back then if he didn't catch enough, well then maybe one night you and your brothers you went hungry. Don't you remember? Of course not!" he said, leaning back in his chair. "Because that was long ago, and one forgets the past so quickly."

"Papa, all of us here can be grateful to this land for all it has given us. But now it is giving us something else. A chance to have a life we never dreamed of. Papa, a man or a woman clinging to a life jacket, they do not keep clinging to it after they have been taken from the sea and are on dry land. Not even when that life jacket has saved their lives. We are free now. As Juanma said, we have a choice."

"A *choice?*" Aurelio's voice now was dripping with sarcasm. "Well then, go on, tell me something.

This 'choice' you talk about, this great choice, what if your son wanted not to be a Catholic, hmm? What if he came home one day and told you that he wanted, let's say, to be a Protestant? Or an atheist? Then what? What would you say to him? That would be all right with you? Will his *faith* also be something he has to choose?"

Concha answered slowly and deliberately.

"He will do what he thinks is right. In the town, he will read many books. He will meet many people, make many friends who will believe many things. They will tell him about these things. And yes, Papa, he will have a choice. But," she said, "my son is a good boy. One day he will grow up to be a good man. And he will make the right choice."

"She's right, Papa." said Juanma.

The old man laughed.

"You fool yourselves, you two. You fool yourselves about what life would be like in the town. You see it like in a dream, but the dream it is not the life."

"Papa," Concha pleaded, "can't you see? Jorge now is like a young plant, growing every day. Soon this pot he's growing in will be too small for him. Unless he is transplanted to a bigger pot, he will not grow."

"You're wrong! You talk about transplanting Jorge? Don't be such fools. The truth is you would be pulling him out by his roots! And do you know what will happen to him then? Hmm? Well, do you? I will tell you. He will grow up always looking out of the corner of his eyes. Because that is how men look in the cities. Is that what you two want? Tell me," he shouted. "Is it? I swear to you, mark my word, if you move him to the town, well then by the time he grows up he will not trust any man. And that will be a good thing, too. Because in the town, men are not to be trusted!"

"Papa..."

"When he is older," Aurelio shouted, slamming his fist on the table, "wine like this will not be good enough for him. He will want to drink rum. Or whiskey. And smoke American cigarettes. He'll stay out all night with his so-called friends. Maybe he'll take drugs. Who knows, we'll have to wait and see what he decides. And if he decides to be a drug addict? Or an atheist? I suppose you do nothing, eh? Is that what you want? Well, is it? Is that the 'new way?' Is that your 'good news?'"

"Papa..."

"No!"

"Papa, please..."

"I said, no! I don't want to hear anymore!"

"Papa, listen to me..."

"I've heard enough!"

Aurelio pushed his chair back from the table and stood.

"This life," he said, "and our little *cortijo*, they are all I ever wanted for myself, for my son, and for my son's family. I can see now, though, that it was not enough. I'm sorry, Juanma. Really, I'm sorry. Your Mama and me, we did the best we could. Honestly we did. You two, or rather you three, you can go wherever and whenever you like. I cannot stop you. But this... this is my home, and I am not going to leave it. What's more, this land is in my name, and I will not let you sell it. But," he added, "I am old, and I will be gone from here soon enough. You can wait a little, I think. And after I'm gone, well then you two can do whatever you want. Jorge is your son, and you will raise him however you see fit. But I will tell you something," he said, his eyes now wandering around the room, "It will be very sad for him if I should die while he is still a boy, and you two then go raise him in the town." He glanced toward the fireplace in the comer. "Because in the town, when they want light at night? They just throw a switch. And when they want heat? They throw another switch. And the children, they grow up never even seeing, never knowing, how beautiful and how magical the world looks like by firelight."

Aurelio turned and left the room.

For a while after he had gone no one said anything. Jorge sat staring at the floor. Juanma and Concha looked at each other.

"What are we going to do?" Concha asked finally.

Juanma leaned forward against the table, wrung his hands together and shook his head.

"I don't know," he said. "I don't know."

THY WILL BE DONE

After leaving the kitchen, Aurelio stood outside for some moments not quite sure what to do or where to go. Finally he made his way up the pathway and along the wall until he came to his special spot. As he had earlier, he took the piece of cardboard out of his rear pocket, laid it across the smoothest stone and sat. Though the afternoon sun was still high, that portion of the wall on which he sat was already in the shade. The stones had been in the sun all day and were still hot, and he could feel the heat through the cardboard.

The workmen on the Punta were still taking their

midday break. Many were sitting on a cluster of rocks eating sandwiches and passing around bottles of wine. The great yellow bulldozer stood stilent.

Looking down the hill toward the sea, Aurelio could make out the little cove where he and his brother Manuel had learned to swim when they were boys. Every Sunday during the summer their father would take them down the trail and along the Punta to the rocky beach. Once there, he would promise an orange and a candy to the first boy who could swim out to the end of the Punta and back. Then their father would sit on the rocks and watch them race. When they had finished they would run up to him, one or the other claiming victory. Then their father would produce an orange for them both, but not a sweet. Only the fastest boy would get the sweet.

Aurelio was a year older than his brother and so he would usually win. Once he remembered he let his brother win, and somehow his father must have understood that, because after Manuel had received his sweet and turned away, their father had put his hand on Aurelio's shoulder and winked at him. That seemed as good as, if not even better than, a sweet.

Aurelio's father's name was Juan. He had lived

to see his son marry, but died before Juanma was born. Later that same year the Civil War broke out, and Manuel was killed fighting in the hills below Granada. Aurelio had better luck, and so later when Juanma was born he was christened "Juan Manuel" for both the grandfather and the uncle he would never know.

Aurelio closed his eyes now, remembering his wife's young face as the two of them had sat up in bed one night picking out the name. Aurelio had wanted their first child to be named Juan, or Juana if it was a girl, and save Manuel for a second child. His wife liked the sound of the two together, and as it turned out that was just as well, for there had never been a second child. Some problem with his wife's "plumbing," the doctor called it.

Opening his eyes once again, Aurelio turned his head and glanced down at those places along the wall where the stones were coming loose. Many had already fallen into scattered piles on the ground. *Nothing lasts forever anymore*, he thought, remembering a time when everything used to feel so permanent. A stone wall... their life there. What happened?

Concha was right about one thing. The world was changing. Looking toward the Punta, he could see how it had already changed so much. It was not easy to watch all these changes. For a moment, Aurelio felt ashamed as he wondered if it hadn't been Manuel who was the lucky one.

Back inside the kitchen, Juanma and Concha were still sitting at the table. Neither was eating. Only Jorge ate. When he was finished he looked up.

"Can I go outside now?"

Juanma and Concha both nodded. Jorge slipped out of his chair and ran out. When he was gone, Juanma turned to his wife.

"Did you see his face?"

"I saw."

"You know why my father left when he did? Because he did not want us to see his tears."

"I know. What are we going to do?"

"My father has not cried since the day he buried my mother. What have I done?"

"You've done *nothing!* Nothing wrong, anyway. He was not crying because of you, Juanma. It was because he knows what we told him is true. He'll think about it. And after he has, he will see it for himself. He just needs a little time, that's all. A few hours maybe, to think about it."

"I don't think so."

"Listen to me! You talked to him about having a choice. But the truth is, we don't have a choice. The choice has been made for us."

"What are you talking about?"

"Okay, yes, we have a little choice maybe. We can say 'No' today. And maybe tomorrow. But sooner or later, you know it's going to happen. If not for fifteen million, then sixteen. Or seventeen. Sooner or later, they will get what they want. You know they will. Because do you really think they will let one man, or one family, stand in their way? No! Never! They have too much at stake. They are strong. Very strong. Even if we wanted to, we could not stop them."

"We cannot sell without his permission. The land is in his name."

"Yes," said Concha, standing up and pacing nervously. "And that gives him the power, doesn't it? He does not want to lose that power, Juanma. Because he thinks it's the only power he has left. We must convince him, *you* must convince him, that if we move into town he will have even *more* power."

"What are you talking about? That's stupid."

"Listen to me. You must make him see that the

past is really the past, and the future is the future. And that future will come either in spite of him, or *because* of him. He has it in his power now to change the world! *Our* world. And *Jorge's* world. And *that* is real power."

"Chita, my father cannot see the future. He cannot even see the present. All he sees is what has been before. I cannot convince him of anything. He must convince himself. And to do that, I think he is going to need some time."

"What are you saying?"

"It's not only giving up this house, or this land. What he's afraid of really is giving up his life. Despite his faith, he is afraid of dying."

"What does selling our land have to do with his dying?"

"Because as long as we are here on the *cortijo,* he knows he has a future. He knows tomorrow the goats must be milked, and he must be the one to milk them. He knows if it rains there will be mushrooms to pick, and that if he, with Jorge's help, does not pick them, well then they will not be picked, because you and I, we already have more work than we can do. So being here makes him feel like he matters...because he *does* matter. We *do* need him.

"But in the town," Juanma continued, "in the life like what we described, okay, yes, he can work. But that would be for *his* sake, not ours. And he knows that. If we had all that money, Chita, he would not really need to work. And so if it was true or not, he would feel useless."

"But..."

"One other thing. Here, every stone, every tree, every sound reminds him of his mother and his father and his brother. If he dies and we are living here still, well then he knows it would be the same for us, that we would be reminded of him always…by everything. But if he dies and we are living in the town? Concha, maybe he is afraid of being forgotten."

"Listen to me," begged Concha. She was desperate. She knew that without Juanma's help there would be no way to change the old man's mind. "Always one is afraid of what one does not know. Besides, he would *not* be useless! He would be helping you in the shop! And…and…when Jorge came home from school? He could...he could..." She was trying so hard to think of something that Aurelio would need to do around the house.

Juanma shook his head.

"No. We have already said all we can to him. He must have time now to think about this."

"How *much* time?"

"I don't know. As much as he needs. I don't want to bring it up again. We'll wait. And then, if he hasn't said anything to us in a month or two..."

"A *month!*" Concha shouted. "Juanma, *what about Jorge? What about his future?*"

Juanma pushed his chair back from the table and stood.

"Juanma, please. *I beg you!*"

"We can't do anything, Chita. I cannot do anything, without his blessing. He *must* give us his blessing. I'll go into town tomorrow and tell Vicente we need more time."

Concha bit down on her lip so hard that she broke the skin.

Juanma walked across the room and disappeared outside.

Jorge was sitting on the wall next to his grandfather, dangling his legs. Neither spoke.

"Are you still angry, Abuelito?" Jorge asked finally.

"No. I am not angry."

"You shouldn't have said that word. Mama

doesn't like it."

"You are right. I should not have said that word. I'm sorry."

The old man put his arm around Jorge.

"Look at us!" he said. "Now *you* are the teacher, and I am the student."

"Abuelito?"

"Yes?"

"Are we going to sell our *cortijo*?"

"I don't know. Not right now. But, maybe later."

"Then will we buy another *cortijo*, in the town?"

"There are no *cortijos* in the town. Only houses and apartments."

"Are there houses like ours?"

"No, they are different. They are newer. And they don't have any land around them."

"No land? Well then, where does one put the barn?"

"There are no barns."

"Then would we have to keep the chickens in the house? And the goats?"

The old man smiled. "In the town, one does not keep animals."

"Then where will we get our milk if we have no goats?"

"Your Mama would buy milk in the store."

"And eggs?"

"She would buy those in the store, too. One can buy anything in the stores."

"Even a *cortijo*?"

The old man looked toward the Punta.

"Yes," he said. "Even a *cortijo*."

"Abuelito, then when I am big and I have lots of money, I will buy you a *cortijo*."

Aurelio looked at his grandson.

"Why, thank you, Jorge. Thank you very much. I will look forward to that."

Through the trees, Aurelio could see Juanma coming toward them. He did not want to face his son just yet, so he was relieved when Juanma did not stop to turn at the wall, but kept going up the path.

"Abuelito?"

"Yes?"

It was Jorge now who looked worried.

"Are you still going to teach me how to whitewash?"

"To tell you the truth, I had forgotten all about it."

"You promised, remember?"

"Yes," said the old man. "I remember. And a

promise is a promise, isn't it?"

Jorge nodded.

"Well, in that case, you will see that I am not the kind of man who breaks a promise. If I told you I will teach you how to whitewash, well then I will teach you how to whitewash!"

Jorge's little eyes sparkled as he clapped his hands in excitement.

"And *then* what, Abuelito? Then what?"

"Then," said the old man, "you and I, we are going to make our house, and our barn, even more beautiful than they already are."

"But, shouldn't we take our siestas first?"

"No. Not today."

"Aren't you tired?"

"Yes," said Aurelio. "I am very tired. So tired, that today I am afraid that if I closed my eyes, I would stay asleep for a very long time. And like we said, a promise is a promise."

Aurelio stood. Jorge hopped down from the wall and took his grandfather's hand. Together they made their way to the barn. At one point the old man tripped and almost fell. Jorge held onto his hand tightly. They kept going. As they approached the barn, Aurelio could see Juanma in the distance leading the two goats into the field next to the almond grove.

He and Jorge stepped inside the barn. Jorge watched Aurelio scoop some lime and chalk out of plastic sacks and put them into an old bucket. The bucket still had patches of dried whitewash left on it from the year before. Then the old man began searching around for a couple of horsehair brushes, two sticks, and some string. He found the brushes and the string right away. They were lying at the back of a shelf, behind a tin full of nails. He crossed to the other side of the barn and searched the ground behind an old barrel. There was a wooden axe handle lying there. His own father had carved it some fifty years before. Alongside it was a *peso romana*, or Roman scale. That had been his grandfather's. Aurelio bent down and picked it up. He brushed it off and tried to work it, but the hinges had long since rusted stiff and wouldn't budge. He tried again. No luck. Then, as if it was still worth saving, he set it back down on the ground and kept looking for the two long sticks. He found them behind a pile of crates. Then he grabbed one of Concha's hand-made brooms that was leaning against the wall.

"Now we have everything we need. So come on,

follow me."

Jorge followed his grandfather back outside, down the pathway and around the house to the three pools. Aurelio then showed Jorge how to mix the lime and chalk with water. Then he carried the bucket over to the side of the house that was in the shade. From inside the house, Concha was watching them through the window.

Using the string that he had just taken from the barn, Aurelio showed Jorge how to tie the brushes onto the ends of the two sticks.

"Like this, you see? So they hold strong."

When he was through, he took the broom and began to sweep the wall of the house.

"We want to paint the wall," he explained. "Not the dirt!"

He was almost finished sweeping when he glanced up and saw Concha staring at him through the window. He kept sweeping. When he was through, he dipped one of the brushes into the bucket of whitewash and began to show Jorge how to spread it on in even strokes.

"Now it doesn't look so beautiful right away because it has to dry. But tomorrow you will see how white it will look. Now go ahead, you try."

"Like *this?*" asked Jorge, splashing some on the wall with his own brush.

"Well, almost," laughed Aurelio. "Only you're getting more on the ground than on the wall. Though I must say, a white ground is a beautiful idea. Still, watch me again carefully. See how I do it?"

Again he dipped his brush into the whitewash, then swung the brush over and onto the wall.

Then Jorge tried it.

"*That's* the idea!" said Aurelio. "You're a natural! Now then, you paint down here, and I will paint up there, and in no time at all..."

"...the house," cried Jorge, "will be even more beautiful than it already is!"

"You got it!"

Concha was no longer watching. She was sitting at the kitchen table. She was holding her stomach, sickened by the thought that Aurelio now was preparing the house for yet another year ahead. There was no point, she knew, in running out to find Juanma to tell him what the old man was doing. He would just tell her again that his father needed more time.

After some moments, Concha took out her pencil and started to make a list of all the things she wanted to say to her husband, and to his father. But then she stopped. There was nothing new. She had said everything that she could think of already.

The goats were chewing anything they could reach in the little field beside the almond grove. A red viper lay coiled in the rocks at the edge of the field. Juanma dragged the last remaining branches from the olive trees into two big piles. One pile of the thicker branches would be cut into pieces later to be used as firewood. The second pile was of branches that were

too small to be of use. He sprinkled some gasoline on those, and lit them. Standing to the windward side of the pile then, he watched as the flames took.

Not knowing what else to do, Concha gathered some leaves of palma plants, took them into the kitchen, and made a new broom. When she was through, she crossed "Make broom" off her list. Then she headed up toward the barn to feed the chickens. Jorge saw her and cried out.

"Mama, look! Abuelito is teaching me how to whitewash!"

"I see," she yelled back, not stopping.

"Come look, Mama."

Concha kept her eyes straight ahead and pretended not to hear him.

The sun was just above the Punta now. Jorge and Aurelio had managed to finish one side of the house, and were hoping to finish a second side before losing what was left of the light. The shadows were growing longer. For a while both worked without saying anything. Then Jorge suddenly stopped, and looked at his grandfather.

"Abuelito?"

"Yes?"

“What’s an astronaut?”

Aurelio thought about it.

“Ah, well, that’s...somebody who goes to the stars.”

Jorge’s face tightened.

“How do they get there?”

“In rockets.”

“What’s a rocket?”

“A special kind of airplane.”

"Oh."

And then a moment later, "The stars are very far away, aren't they?"

"Very."

"So does it take them a long time to get there?"

"I don't know. I suppose it does."

Aurelio waited for the next question. When it didn't come, he resumed brushing.

"Abuelito?"

"Yes?"

"What do they do when they get there?"

"They take pictures."

"Why?"

"Well…to see, I guess, if the stars are as pretty as they thought."

"And? Are they?"

"I suppose they are."

"Have you seen the pictures, Abuelito?"

"No. But I have heard about them."

"How old do you have to be to be an astronaut?"

"I don't know," said the old man.

"Very old?"

"I tell you something," said Aurelio. "These are questions maybe you had better ask your mother. She seems to know all about these things."

Jorge nodded. He dipped his brush back into the bucket, and went back to work. A moment later though he stopped again.

"Abuelito?"

"Yes?"

"When I am old enough, do you think maybe I can be a farmer *and* an astronaut?"

The shadows along the side of the house were growing darker quickly. On the Punta, the bulldozer again stood silent. The workmen had stopped working, and were getting on their motorbikes and heading home. Aurelio decided it was time that he and Jorge also call it a day.

Jorge was splattered head to toe with whitewash. He helped his grandfather rinse the brushes and the bucket in the runoff from the lower pool. They were putting them away by the side of the house when Concha appeared on the patio.

"Jorge?"

"Yes, Mama?"

"I want you to change your clothes and wash up

before supper."

"But Mama, I'm helping Abuelito."

"I said, come with me."

The little boy looked up at his grandfather.

"It's alright," said the old man. "Do like your Mama says. I can finish here alone."

Reluctantly, Jorge turned and went into the house. Aurelio watched him go. Then he took an old rag and began to wipe away some of the whitewash that had spilt onto the patio. He was on his hands and knees when Juanma came around the corner leading the mule to water. The two men looked at each other. They didn't say anything. Juanma led the mule to the spring.

Aurelio finished mopping up, and then washed himself. He made his way around the house, and up the pathway to his wall. Once again he headed for his special spot, and just as his day had begun so it ended.

The day seemed to hold its ground for a while, until at last it started to fade and night moved in. The shadows of the olive trees stretched out across the field until they began to run into one another. Birds darted back and forth catching insects, while across the bay at Torrenueva the street lights came on automatically.

In the distance just above the horizon there was

a gray haze made up of dust borne by winds that had come out of the south from Africa. Above it, the sky was still a pale blue though turning darker quickly. Here and there a rose-colored cloud still drifted overhead. A high altitude jet passed over the Punta leaving behind it a vapor trail that looked like a long straight cloud.

At last the sun slipped behind the Punta. Its light still reflected off the clouds onto the sea below, and the water, deep and smooth, took on a dull pink sheen. Here and there a fishing boat was heading out. One of those moved beyond the shadow of the Punta. It caught the last of the day's light. Another of the boats slipped close to shore. Aurelio watched as the fisherman dropped his net beside the seawall that edged the urbanization. The water there was deep where they had dredged a harbor for the new marina. It was a good place to fish.

To his left, lights were coming on in Cotobro, another new development. Suddenly Aurelio remembered something that his mother used to tell him. When he would complain about something, she would look at him and say, "Where there is light there are shadows. And where there are shadows there is light."

Aurelio tried now to imagine the bright side of what Juanma and Concha wanted to do. But he couldn't manage it. He looked again toward the Punta. Beyond it in the distance he could see an oil tanker making its way along the coast. It was heading toward Gibraltar and the open sea beyond. There were so many things out there that Aurelio hadn't seen, and didn't understand.

Now the old man heard the bells that the goats wore around their necks. He turned and saw the silhouettes of Juanma and both goats as they moved past the trees back toward the barn. Aurelio looked up at the sky. One by one the stars were beginning to appear. Jorge's words from that afternoon came rushing into his head. *Abuelito, what's an astronaut?...What do they do when they get to the stars?...When I am old enough, can I be a farmer AND an astronaut?*

Aurelio shook his head. The words kept repeating, and seemed to grow louder. He tried looking away from the stars. It didn't help. The words kept getting louder still. They grew so loud that the old man felt dizzy. Now the stars were spinning and coming closer. He tried closing his eyes, but that only made it worse. It felt like he was going to fall. He reached out with both hands to brace himself. His breathing grew more difficult. And suddenly he was so afraid...that by trying to keep Jorge on the *cortijo* he was not, as was his dream, *giving* the boy the stars, but instead maybe he was even taking them away.

He knew nothing of this "new world" about which they had talked. The world of men and women traveling through space, with their computers and all their new ideas. Those were like fantasies to him. And yet, it did seem possible that the world was growing bigger, not smaller as he feared. Anything was possible these days. One only had to look as far as the Punta to see the way in which men even changed the shape of mountains to suit their fancy.

The dizziness eased off. Aurelio closed his eyes once again. This time it was to pray. Suddenly the line between right and wrong had blurred. Like a path that was overgrown. He wasn't sure which way to turn.

And then he saw his wife. She was older than when he had imagined her earlier in the day. She looked now as she did just before she died. Every detail so clear. The soft gray hair. The gentle face. The smile. And those eyes. It was as if she was actually sitting right next to him on the wall. The chill that he had been feeling left him. Instead, he felt a slow warmth come over him.

They sat together for some time. The old man actually spoke. He didn't mean to. It was as if his thoughts leaked out of him in whispers. After a while he didn't even mind it. It felt perfectly natural. After all, he was able to imagine her voice, so it seemed only right that she should be able to hear his, too. And then suddenly he felt a calm come over him. His mind cleared. And when the image of his wife left him, Aurelio knew what he had to do.

It was dark and still around the house as he stepped onto the patio. Someone had made a fire in the kitchen. Wisps of smoke were rising from the chimney over the house. A yellow kerosene light shone through the window. Aurelio stepped inside. Concha was saying something to Juanma, but at the sight of Aurelio she stopped. Jorge looked up at his grandfather but did not say anything.

Juanma was kneeling next to the fire. Concha and Jorge were already seated at the table. The room was warm, and smelled of wood smoke. The light from the fire flickered on the walls and on the ceiling, and on all their faces.

Aurelio sat. Juanma joined them. They ate slowly and in silence. Then Juanma asked Jorge about his day. Jorge told him about the snails, and the mushrooms, and how his grandfather had taught him how to whitewash. And about the big lizard he had seen on a rock behind the barn. At last when they were through eating Aurelio finally spoke.

"I have an announcement," he said.

The others all looked at him.

"What you two were talking about earlier was the future," he said. "I am seventy-six years old. And because of that, I do not really have so much of a future left. Not here, anyway. It will not be long, Juanma, before your mother and I, we are together again."

"Papa, I…"

"Let me finish. Speaking of your mother, she was a very wise woman. And so this evening, when I was sitting outside on the wall, I imagined that she was sitting with me. And we had a little talk, she and me. You will laugh maybe, but I asked her what she would do. And you know what she said?"

"No, Papa. What did she say?"

"She said the same thing, Concha, that you said earlier about your son. She said 'My son is a good boy. He has become a good man. And if he is given the choice, he will do the right thing.'"

"Jorge is your son," Aurelio continued. "Therefore, you two must raise him like you see fit. And I do not wish to interfere. Not in your future, and not in his. So, Juanma, I have decided it is not for me to say yes or no. This decision is yours to make. And whatever you decide, I will respect it."

"You are a good man, Juanma. You have been a good son, and you are a good father. Whatever you decide it will not be easy for you. But it is in your hands now, and so you must do what you think is right."

The old man stood.

"Now, if you will excuse me," he said, "I am very tired. It has been a long day, and I would like to go to sleep."

He turned and left the room.

No one said anything. Jorge was so tired that he had already fallen asleep in his chair.

Juanma and Concha just sat there.Then finally, still without saying anything, Juanma swung his chair around to face the fire.

Concha stood up and cleared the table. Then she crossed to her husband and put a hand on his shoulder.

"Are you coming to bed?" she asked.

"In a while," said Juanma. He was staring into the flames. Concha walked over to Jorge.

"Come on my little one," she whispered, lifting

him into her arms. “You’ve had a long day, haven’t you?”

And with that, holding him tightly she carried her son from the room.

PalmArtPress

Michael Lederer
Das Große Spiel, The Great Game
Berlin-Warschau-Express und andere Geschichten
ISBN: 978-3-941524-13-2 German, 280 Pages
ISBN: 978-3-941524-27-9 G (eBook)
ISBN: 978-3-941524-12-5 English, 242 Pages
Short Stories, Softcover, 14,8 x 21 cm

Anne Lorquet-Leithäuser
Kirschenzeiten
ISBN: 978-3-941524-17-0 German,
ISBN: 978-3-941524-35-4 G (eBook)
Novel, 299 Pages, Softcover, 14,8 x 21 cm

Wolfgang Nieblich
Der Hecht im Schulranzen
ISBN: 978-3-941524-08-8
ISBN: 978-3-941524-18-7 (eBook)
192 Pages, 168 Colour Illustr., Hardcover, 16,5 x 23,5 cm

Wolfgang Nieblich
Das Ferne so nah oder **Die Currywurst**
ISBN: 978-3-941524-09-5
ISBN: 978-3-941524-29-3 (eBook)
64 Pages, 18 Colour Illustr., Hardcover, 8 x 10 cm

Sladjana Lukic
Deutsche Grammatik- ***leicht gemacht***
ISBN: 978-3-941524-04-0
Reference, 216 Pages, Softcover, 16,5 x 23,5 cm

Maria Reinecke
Leben in den Zwischenräumen, Living In Between
ISBN: 978-3-941524-21-7 German, 182 Pages
ISBN: 978-3-941524-23-1 G (eBook)
ISBN: 978-3-941524-22-4 English, 172 Pages
ISBN: 978-3-941524-24-8 E (eBook)
Novel, Softcover, 12 x 18 cm

Wolfgang Nieblich
Wahr oder Nicht wahr
Kurzgeschichten und Berichte
ISBN: 978-3-941524-14-9
ISBN: 978-3-941524-28-6 (eBook)
Anthology, 266 Pages, Softcover, 12 x 18 cm

Michael Kromarek
KunstGeschichten *ernst und heiter*
ISBN: 978-3-941524-11-8
ISBN: 978-3-941524-19-4 (eBook)
Short Stories, 150 Pages, Softcover, 12 x 18 cm

Maria Reinecke
La Rambla- *Barcelona Story*
ISBN: 978-3-941524-20-0 English, 96 Pages
ISBN: 978-3-941524-24-5 E (eBook)
ISBN: 978-3-941524-02-6 German, 76 Pages
ISBN: 978-3-941524-26-2 G (eBook)
Short Story, Softcover, 12 x 18 cm

To order: www.palmartpress.com
Postage and handling within Germany is free of charge.